PLAYDATE PALS

Sheep is
SCARED

Rosie Greening • Dawn Machell

make
believe
ideas

Sheep was feeling **tired**.

He had been playing with his friends
all day, and it was time for bed.

One by one, **Sheep's** friends fell asleep.

First Hippo . . .   then Alligator . . .

Sheep looked around. Everything seemed **different** in the dark.

The beds looked different, the room sounded different, and worst of all, **Sheep felt different**.

His heart began **beating** very hard,
and he started to **shake**.

Sheep saw something under Hippo's bed.
It was big, dark, and **monster-shaped**!

"Oh, no! Maybe there is a monster under my bed too!" **whispered** Sheep, and he **hugged** his blanket tightly.

Suddenly there was a loud **BANG**!

The **noise** made **Sheep jump**, and his tummy felt all **squiggly**.

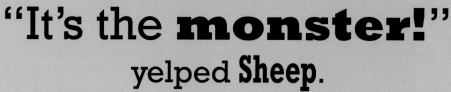

"It's the **monster!**"
yelped Sheep.

Hippo heard **Sheep** and woke up.
Then Hippo turned on the light.

Sheep felt a little less **scared** now
that the room looked normal again, but
he didn't want to **let go** of his blanket.

"What's the matter, **Sheep**?" asked Hippo.

Sheep told them about the monster and
his friends looked under Hippo's bed.

It wasn't a monster –
it was Hippo's boots!

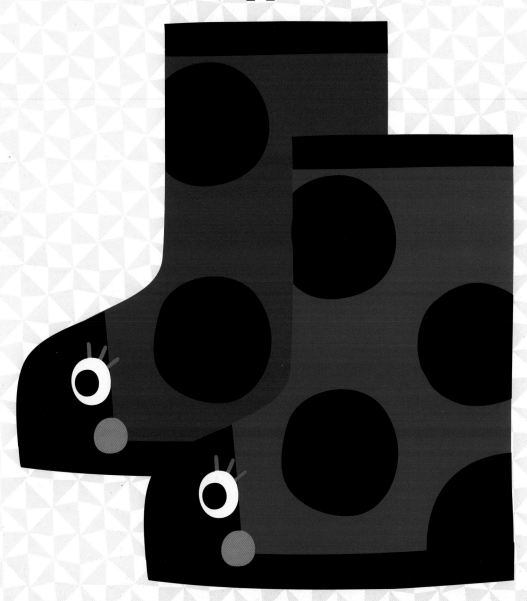

Then **Sheep** remembered
the **banging noises**.

Hippo opened the curtains.
It wasn't a monster – it was a storm!

The thunder **BOOMED**, and **Sheep jumped**.

Hippo **hugged** Sheep. "Don't worry, **Sheep**.
Everyone gets **scared** sometimes,
but we'll take care of you."

After that, **Sheep** felt a lot **happier**,
so the friends went back to bed.

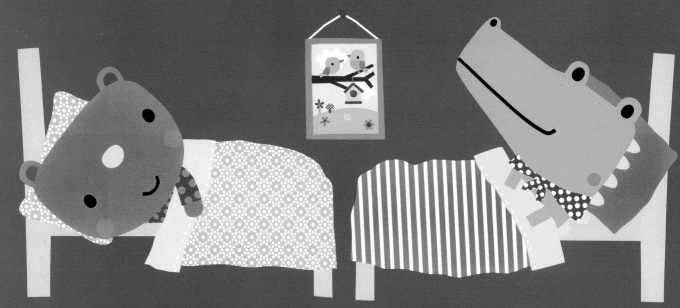

This time, **Sheep** had no trouble getting to sleep!

When **Sheep** woke up
the next morning,
he felt **happy**
and **safe**.

The sun was shining, so the animals
put on their boots and went outside.

The rain had made lots of lovely puddles to jump in!

Sheep had lots of **fun** playing with his friends.

READING TOGETHER

Playdate Pals have been written for parents, caregivers, and teachers to share with young children who are beginning to explore the feelings they have about themselves and the world around them.

Each story is intended as a springboard to emotional discovery and can be used to gently promote further discussion around the feeling or behavioral topic featured in the book.

Sheep is Scared is designed to help children recognize their own feelings of fear and how they behave when they are frightened. Once you have read the story together, go back and talk about any experiences the children might share with Sheep. Practice talking about your feelings together and encourage children to do so in other trusted relationships.

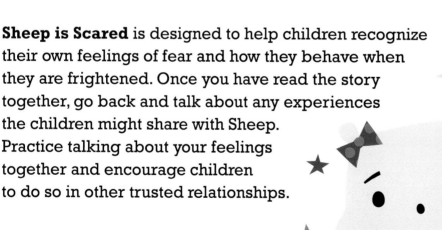

Look at the pictures

Talk about the characters. Are they smiling, frowning, hiding, or jumping? Help children think about what people look like or how they move their bodies when they are scared.

Words in bold

Throughout each story there are words highlighted in bold type. These words specify either the **character's name** or useful words and phrases relating to feeling **scared.** You may wish to put emphasis on these words or use them as reminders for parts of the story you can return to and discuss.

Questions you can ask

To prompt further exploration of this feeling, you could try asking children some of the following questions:

- What makes you feel scared and how do you show it?
- When you are scared, what does it feel like in your body?
- What do you feel like doing when you are scared?
- Can you make a scared face?